A MESSAGE TO PARENTS

It is of vital importance for parents to read good books to young children in order to aid the child's psychological and intellectual development. At the same time as stimulating the child's imagination and awareness of his environment, it creates a positive relationship between parent and child. The child will gradually increase his basic vocabulary and will soon be able to read books alone.

Brown Watson has published this series of books with these aims in mind. By collecting this inexpensive library, parent and child are provided with hours of pleasurable and profitable reading.

© 1995 Brown Watson
ENGLAND
Printed and bound in Germany

Teddy's
Moon Balloon

by Maureen Spurgeon
Illustrated by Pamela Storey

Brown Watson
ENGLAND

One morning, Teddy Bear had just eaten his porridge, when – guess what he saw through the window? A big, yellow balloon! A big, yellow balloon with a ticket tied to the string! Teddy watched it bouncing and bobbing along as the breeze lifted it up into the sky. There were lots of other balloons, too!

"There's a balloon race in the meadow today, Teddy," smiled Daddy Bear. "It's to raise money for the toys' hospital."
"Balloon race?" said Teddy. "What's that?" So Daddy explained.

"Every bear who buys a balloon writes their name on a ticket. And when the balloons go up in the air, the bear whose name is on the balloon which goes the furthest, wins the race!"

Teddy wanted a big, yellow balloon like the one he had seen outside his window! By the time his turn came to put his name on a ticket, there was only one left. Teddy did like its round, smiley face!

It was such a lovely, big, smiley balloon that Teddy didn't want to let go of the string. Then a gust of wind tugged it out of his paw and away it went, up and up, higher and higher into the sky.

"When's the race over?" he asked.
"When we know which balloon
has travelled the furthest," said
Mummy. "So if your balloon goes
further than anyone else's you win
a prize!"

"But my balloon WILL come back,"
he said anxiously. "Won't it?"
"Maybe," said Daddy at last. "If
you wish hard enough!" So, for
the rest of the day, Teddy kept
wishing and wishing.

Teddy just could not stop thinking about his big, yellow balloon with the smiley face. And as it grew dark, he stared up at the sky, hoping he might just see it again.

"Bedtime, Teddy!" said Daddy Bear.

"Want to see something big and yellow, with a smiley face?"
"My balloon?" gasped Teddy.
"Not quite," smiled Daddy. "But you're nearly right!"

"It's the Man in the Moon!" Daddy went on. "Isn't he like your balloon?" Teddy smiled and nodded. And the more he looked at the Man in the Moon, the nearer his smiley face seemed to get . . .

Suddenly, Teddy sat up, his eyes big and round. "YOU'RE not the Man in the Moon!" he cried, staring at the smiling face. "You're my big, yellow balloon!"

The balloon smiled and bobbed about. Teddy reached out to grab the string – and the next minute, he was sailing through the window, with the balloon lifting him up and up into the night sky!

"This is fun!" Teddy laughed.
And so it was. Lots of balloons were doing their best to be in the race. But none of them could catch Teddy and his big, yellow, smiley balloon!

And the closer they got to the Man in the Moon, the bigger his round, yellow face became! "The winner!" he declared, in his deep, rumbly sort of voice. "Teddy Bear has won the balloon race!"

The balloon lifted Teddy Bear a tiny
bit higher, then they floated down
on a soft cloud. The Man in the
Moon's smile was so bright, it was
almost like daytime – except for the
stars twinkling!

"What's this?" asked Teddy, holding out his paw towards a shower of beautiful silver balls drifting down. "Is it rain?"
"No!" chuckled the cloud. "They are moonbeams! Look!"

The cloud gave a little puff and a silver moonbeam floated onto Teddy's paw. "That's for winning the balloon race!" said the cloud. "And for coming to see ME!" boomed the Man in the Moon.

Before Teddy could speak, there was a flash in the sky, then a rumble, strong enough to shake the cloud. "I knew there'd be a storm," puffed the cloud, "as soon as my edges turned black!"

"Time for you to go, Teddy Bear!"
said the Man in the Moon. "Will
you come and see me again?"
"Ooh, yes!" said Teddy, putting
the moonbeam in his pocket.
"Thank you very much!"

The big, yellow balloon gave a little
tug on its string, taking Teddy Bear
up into the air once more. Thunder
rolled and the lightning flashed –
but Teddy didn't mind, not one bit!

Very soon, Teddy was back in his bed, with the big, yellow balloon smiling at him and the Man in the Moon playing Hide-and-Seek behind the clouds. Teddy watched him for a long time before he fell asleep.

"Quite a storm we had last night, Teddy!" said Mummy Bear next day. "My – my balloon!" cried Teddy, looking at the empty space at the end of his bed. "My big, yellow balloon!"

Daddy laughed. "You're going to get it back after all, Teddy! Your balloon went the furthest and you've won the balloon race! What a splendid prize you've got!"

Teddy's prize was a journey in a real balloon! Up into the sky he went, his friends cheering and waving. And how different it all looked in the daytime!